Text copyright © 2004 by Kate Banks
Pictures copyright © 2004 by Georg Hallensleben
All rights reserved
Distributed in Canada by Douglas & McIntyre Ltd.
Color separations by Hong Kong Scanner Arts
Printed and bound in the United States of America by Berryville Graphics
Designed by Nancy Goldenberg
First edition, 2004
10 9 8 7 6 5 4 3 2 1

Library of Congress Cataloging-in-Publication Data
Banks, Kate, 1960–
    The cat who walked across France / Kate Banks ; pictures by
Georg Hallensleben.— 1st ed.
        p.   cm.
    Summary: After his owner dies, a cat wanders across the countryside
of France, unable to forget the home he had in the stone house by the
edge of the sea.
    ISBN 0-374-39968-9
    [1. Cats—Fiction.   2. Home—Fiction.   3. France—Fiction.]
I. Hallensleben, Georg, ill.   II. Title.

PZ7.B22594 Cat 2003
[E]—dc21
                                                    2002025091

The Cat Who Walked Across France

KATE BANKS

pictures by GEORG HALLENSLEBEN

Frances Foster Books

Farrar, Straus and Giroux • New York

For many years the cat had lived in the stone house by the edge of the sea.

He chased the wind that scuttled through the garden.

He watched the birds flitter from tree to tree.

At dusk he curled up in the bend of the old woman's arm.

The old woman would scratch the cat's ears and stroke his back.

"Good kitty, good kitty."

Then one day the old woman died.
Her belongings, along with the cat, were shipped north,
to the house where she was born.

But there was no one to scratch the cat's ears or stroke his back.
And soon the cat was forgotten.

He prowled the streets begging for scraps to eat and fleeing from stray dogs.

Until one day he left.

He roamed the countryside, circling pastures
where animals grazed.
And he watched his own shadow lengthen
as each day drew to a close.
At night he sheltered himself in a lonely barn.
He lay in a pile of stiff hay.
But when he closed his eyes, he could feel
the softness of the bluegrass that grew behind
the stone house by the edge of the sea.

At daybreak the cat would bathe himself
in the first rays of the sun. Then he would trot off.
Sometimes he strolled. Other times he slunk.
He learned to hunt field mice and birds and drink from village fountains.
Once someone set a bowl of milk under his nose,
and he thought of staying. But then a voice cried, "Run along now."

Big cities loomed large,
bustling and brimming with noise.
But the cat scampered bravely down the wide avenues,
dodging cars and bicycles.

Children playing ball would chase after him or cry, "Shoo, shoo!"
And the cat would scurry up a tree.

But when he nestled in its branches, he would remember
the tangy smell of lemons ripening on a branch under a window
at the stone house by the edge of the sea. And he would move on.

The cat pranced over bridges and bristled at the thundering trains
that passed. At dusk he would lick the dirt from his face and paws.
In his dreams he could hear the twigs snapping
and the crunch of dried leaves as he circled around
the stone house by the edge of the sea.

Weeks passed. Then months.
The cat measured time against
the weathered soles of his feet.
His fur grew scruffy.
Now and again he would stop to linger
on a grassy bank or in the cool shade of an ancient wall.

Or he would pause to watch a barge
gliding down a canal.

When it rained, the cat took refuge under a friendly rafter.
He was lonely and tired. But when the storm passed, he would march on,
driven by the taste of the salty air that blew off the water and coated
the bench behind the stone house by the edge of the sea.

When the cat came to a river, he would stop for a drink. He would watch the fish jump in wide arcs over the water, and he would cry, "Meow!" Then he would stretch his legs, arch his back, and continue on his way.

Sometimes he stopped to romp in the fields.
He rolled in the tall grass and skipped over buttercups.
But when he came to the fields of lavender, a memory stirred, and
the cat saw the blue door of the stone house by the edge of the sea
and the soft light in the hallway that seemed to say, "Come right in."

The cat was thin and frail when he wandered into the port.
The boats with their flapping sails told him he was nearby.

At last he walked up to the gate of the stone house by the edge of the sea.
The front door was wide open.
The cat walked in. He settled into a warm spot and fell asleep.

He awoke to the sound of voices.

"Where did it come from? Do you suppose it's lost?"

A boy and a girl were standing over him, talking.

A platter of food was set on the floor. And a bowl of fresh water.

The cat shied away.

"Here, kitty," said a soft voice.

A hand reached under the cat's chin and scratched.

The cat began to purr. He closed his eyes.

He was reminded of the hands of an old woman stroking his back.

He could hear her quiet breathing and gentle words: "Good kitty."

And he knew he was home.